Dear Parents and Educators,

Welcome to Penguin Young Readers! As parents and educators, you know that each child develops at his or her own pace—in terms of speech, critical thinking, and, of course, reading. Penguin Young Readers recognizes this fact. As a result, each Penguin Young Readers book is assigned a traditional easy-to-read level (1–4) as well as a Guided Reading Level (A–P). Both of these systems will help you choose the right book for your child. Please refer to the back of each book for specific leveling information. Penguin Young Readers features esteemed authors and illustrators, stories about favorite characters, fascinating nonfiction, and more!

Please, No More Nuts!

LEVEL **2**

GUIDED READING LEVEL **H**

This book is perfect for a **Progressing Reader** who:
- can figure out unknown words by using picture and context clues;
- can recognize beginning, middle, and ending sounds;
- can make and confirm predictions about what will happen in the text; and
- can distinguish between fiction and nonfiction.

Here are some **activities** you can do during and after reading this book:
- Problem/Solution: In this story, the squirrels have too many nuts and are tired of eating them. What solution do they come up with to solve this problem?
- Rhyming Words: On a separate piece of paper, make a list of all the rhyming words in this story. For example, *eight* rhymes with *plate*, so write those two words next to each other.

Remember, sharing the love of reading with a child is the best gift you can give!

—Sarah Fabiny, Editorial Director
    Penguin Young Readers program

*Penguin Young Readers are leveled by independent reviewers applying the standards developed by Irene Fountas and Gay Su Pinnell in *Matching Books to Readers: Using Leveled Books in Guided Reading*, Heinemann, 1999.

For Carrie, who can always see the positive.
Thank you—JF

PENGUIN YOUNG READERS
An Imprint of Penguin Random House LLC

Penguin supports copyright. Copyright fuels creativity, encourages diverse voices,
promotes free speech, and creates a vibrant culture. Thank you for buying an authorized edition
of this book and for complying with copyright laws by not reproducing, scanning, or distributing any
part of it in any form without permission. You are supporting writers and allowing Penguin to
continue to publish books for every reader.

Copyright © 2018 by Jonathan Fenske. All rights reserved. Published by Penguin Young Readers,
an imprint of Penguin Random House LLC, 345 Hudson Street, New York, New York 10014.
Manufactured in China.

Library of Congress Cataloging-in-Publication Data is available.

ISBN 9780515159653 (pbk)   10 9 8 7 6 5 4 3 2 1
ISBN 9780515159660 (hc)   10 9 8 7 6 5 4 3 2 1

PLEASE, NO MORE NUTS!

by Jonathan Fenske

Penguin Young Readers
An Imprint of Penguin Random House

Take five.
Take six.
Take seven.
Take eight.

6

I used to love nuts.
I ADORED them.

And I'll admit,
I used to hoard them.

I stuffed my brother's chubby cheeks with nuts to keep us fed for weeks.

10

Back THEN I was a nut for nuts.

But NOW I cannot stand their guts.

It's nuts for breakfast.

Nuts for brunch.

Nuts for snack,

and nuts for lunch.

Nuts for supper. EVERY DAY.

Take them! Make them go away!

Nuts in milkshakes.

Nuts in stew.

Nuts to slurp,

and nuts to chew.

14

Nuts on pancakes.

Nuts on pie.

If I eat
ONE MORE NUT
I'll cry!

So many nuts
for YOU to eat!

Nuts for breakfast!

Nuts for brunch!

luts for snack,

and nuts for lunch!

28

**Nuts for supper.
EVERY DAY.**

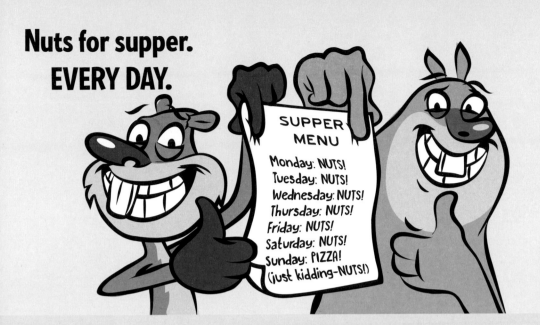

**They're all for YOU!
Hip, hip, HOORAY!**

30